MW01438175

Canyon Ridge High
School Library
Withdrawn

8771 EN
Just Like Everyone Else

Bunting, Eve
ATOS BL 3.5
Points: 1.0

UG

FASTBACK ® Romance

Just Like Everyone Else

EVE BUNTING

MORNINGSIDE SCHOOL LIBRARY

FEARON/JANUS
Belmont, California
Simon & Schuster Supplementary Education Group

FASTBACK® ROMANCE BOOKS
Fifteen
For Always
The Girl in the Painting
Just Like Everyone Else
Maggie the Freak
Nobody Knows But Me
Oh, Rick!
A Part of the Dream
Survival Camp
Two Different Girls

Cover photographer: Richard Hutchings

Cover copyright © 1984 by Fearon/Janus, a division of Simon & Schuster Supplementary Education Group, 500 Harbor Boulevard, Belmont, California 94002. All rights reserved.

Copyright © 1978 by Creative Education, Inc. International copyrights reserved in all countries. No part of this book may be reproduced in any form without written permission from the publisher.

ISBN 0-8224-3529-2

Library of Congress Catalog Card Number: 83-62630

Printed in the United States of America.

2. 15 14 13 12 11 10 9 8 7 6 5 4 3

It was only 6 a.m., and we didn't have to be at the airport until 8:30 that morning. I was trying to eat my breakfast, but Mom and my little sister, Jo-Jo, kept bugging me to hurry.

"It's just that we don't want her getting off the plane in a strange country and not seeing anyone she knows," Mom said. "Get a move on, Eric."

"She doesn't know us," I pointed out. I gobbled down the last of my eggs.

"She" was Maeve, an Irish girl who was coming to spend the summer with us. It was a pretty name. Gaelic, Mom said, and it rhymed with Dave.

"OK, I'm ready," I said. Through the

window I could see Dad, already in the car with the engine running. We were heading for the door when the phone rang.

Jo-Jo ran back and picked it up. "It's for you, Eric," she said. "It's your girlfriend."

Mom frowned. "Tell her you don't have time to talk," she said.

I nodded and took the phone.

"Eric?" Kitty's voice was soft and husky. How could she sound this good so early in the morning?

I swallowed. "Hi."

"Are you ready to go?"

"Just about." I watched Mom tapping the face of her watch.

"Well . . ." Kitty paused. "See you later then. You still think it'll be all right for me to come over?"

I imagined her sitting up in bed to talk to me, her hair hanging in long, sleepy, blonde tangles over her brown shoulders. I swallowed again. "Sure. Come about ten."

"OK. Bye, Eric."

"Is she still trying to butt in?" Jo-Jo asked before Mom managed to shove Jo-Jo ahead of her through the kitchen door. "She's dying to get a look at Maeve," Jo-Jo yelled over her shoulder. "She's afraid Maeve will be cuter than she is."

That showed how much Jo-Jo knew. There was no one cuter than Kitty! I grinned and reached around Mom to yank Jo-Jo's T-shirt out of her jeans. She scowled at me and smoothed it back in.

Dad drove. If I'd been driving we'd have gotten to the airport in no time flat.

I climbed into the back seat next to Jo-Jo and closed my eyes.

"Aren't you even excited about Maeve coming?" Jo-Jo sounded exasperated.

"What for?" I asked. Of course I kind of was. But it wouldn't have been cool to show it. What guy wouldn't be at the thought of a strange 16-year-old girl sharing his house for two months?

Mom was the one who had suggested that Maeve come. She and Dad had gone on their dream vacation to England last summer, and they'd met Maeve's parents there. They had been on vacation, too, from Belfast in North Ireland. From what they'd told Mom and Dad, Belfast was a good place to get away from. They were having something called "the troubles" there, which meant the country was practically in a civil war. There were tanks in the streets, and people were being shot and bombed. I guess Maeve's parents had said how much Maeve wanted to visit the United States, and a half dozen letters later, here she was.

Or here she would be, when her plane arrived.

When her flight was announced, the four of us joined the crowd around the gate and watched the passengers come off. It was a jumbo jet, and the stream seemed never ending. Mom had a snapshot of Maeve, and she kept looking at it and peering through the crowd at every Ms., Miss, or Mrs. who came off the plane.

"She has red hair, Mom, remember?" I said. "That's what her mother said."

"But girls keep changing their hair color these days," Mom muttered. "Oh, why didn't I tell her to wear a carnation?"

When Maeve did finally appear, we all recognized her immediately.

Her hair was red all right. *RED!* And it curled around her face in the biggest natural I'd ever seen. A red natural! And she was tall. *TALL!*

"Wow!" For once Jo-Jo was speechless.

"She looks sick," Dad said. "I mean, the poor girl looks ill."

She sure did. I'd never seen anyone that pale.

"Exhaustion," Mom said. "Nerves." She waved the photograph. "Yoo-hoo, Maeve."

Maeve stood blinking, as if unsure whether to get off or stay on the plane until it turned around and went back to Ireland. She came slowly down the ramp.

"She looks scared to death," Mom said softly. "I don't think the poor little thing has been out of Ireland before."

Little? Come on, Mom.

We waited for her to come through the gates.

As soon as it was possible, Mom rushed at her and smothered her in a hug. "Maeve! We've been so anxious for you to get here."

Dad beamed. "Welcome to California."

I stood back a little. "Hi," I said, and I tried not to stare. That red hair and that white, white face. She wore beige corduroys and a blue sweater, and her eyes were bluer than any eyes I'd ever seen. She was so red, white, and blue she could have been the American flag.

Jo-Jo hung behind Mom, overcome by some new, strange silence.

We picked up Maeve's luggage. She said the suitcases had cleared customs in Chicago. At least, I think that's what she said. Her accent was hard to understand.

"Are you feeling all right, dear?" Mom asked. "You're very pale."

"I am," Maeve said and left it at that while we all stood waiting for more.

People stared at her as we walked to our car. And this was the Los Angeles airport, where the kookiest people in the world hung out. I guess it was all that red hair. I was glad when we got to the car and could hide her.

She sat between Jo-Jo and me while Dad fought the traffic out of the airport.

"There are a terrible lot of motorcars, aren't there?" she ventured once. Once she said shyly, "I can hardly believe that I'm here."

Jo-Jo was gradually getting back to being her normal self. Unfortunately. "Did your house ever get bombed?" she asked.

"Maeve doesn't want to talk about that," Dad said. I could see by her face that Maeve didn't.

"Well, you don't need to worry about bombs over here," Mom said. "You can just relax and enjoy yourself."

"It sounds grand," Maeve said.

Jo-Jo bounced up. "We're home."

We went into the house the back way. Dad and I carried the bags.

Maeve stopped short when she saw our pool. "You don't mean it!" she said. "Sure you must all be millionaires."

"No way," I told her. "There are a bunch of pools on our street. And I've never even seen a millionaire."

"It's because it's California," Dad explained.

I stood beside Maeve, and it was as if I were seeing our backyard for the first time. The blue of the pool, the low cluster of palm trees by the deep end, the cement, which had a few cracks in it since the last earthquake but still looked pretty good, were seen through new eyes.

"You can swim, can't you?" Mom looked anxious, and I knew she had visions of a drowned guest.

"I can indeed," Maeve said. "Can I go in right away? My suit is in there." She pointed to the biggest suitcase.

"Don't you want to rest first?" Mom asked.

"Och, sure, I'm not tired at all," Maeve said.

I changed into my swimsuit and dived into the deep end to wait for her. The water didn't feel like 73 degrees. It always felt cooler at first. I heard the glass door to the den slide open, and Maeve came out with Jo-Jo.

"Come on in," I yelled.

Maeve unbuttoned the blue shirt she was wearing and took it off. Her swimsuit was blue, too, with thin pink stripes. She was white all over. But I decided right then that if she got a California tan, and if she cut 10 inches of her hair and 10 off her legs, she'd be OK-looking. Not terrific, like Kitty. But OK.

She walked down the pool steps the way little kids do. Then she began to swim, and she swam the way little kids do, too. Even Mom could do better than the breast stroke! She kept her chin way up out of the water, and her head with its circle of red hair was like a beach ball bobbing toward me.

She puffed her way halfway up the pool and then grabbed the edge.

"You swim very well, dear," Mom called from the kitchen window.

"I go to the baths a lot," Maeve told me.

"The baths? What are they?" I asked.

"You know. The indoor pool."

"Oh." I tried not to laugh. The water reflected the blue in her eyes. Up close her face and shoulders had the color and smoothness of new snow. The sun struck sparks from her hair, and it seemed that if water touched it, it would sizzle.

"Hi, Kitty," I heard Mom call from the house. I looked away from Maeve and saw Kitty coming through the doorway.

"Hi, Eric. Jo-Jo."

"Oh, shoot," Jo-Jo muttered and jumped into the water.

I pulled myself up over the edge of the pool and dripped my way across to Kitty. Already the cement was hot enough to make me hop. But Kitty was worth hopping for.

"Kitty, this is Maeve," I said.

Maeve took a deep breath and began her slow, puffing breast stroke to the steps. I could tell that Kitty was pretty stunned by all that red hair and all that whiteness rising out of our pool.

Maeve tried to dry her wet hand on her wet suit, and then she shrugged and just smiled at Kitty.

Kitty stood, still staring, and it was the strangest thing. Right there, in front of my eyes, I saw Maeve realize for the first time that she was too tall, too white, too weird. She sort of hunched herself over.

"Hi," Kitty said.

Honest, that was all she said, as I told Mom and Dad afterwards when I was trying to defend her.

"It wasn't what she said," Mom told me furiously. "It was the way she stared at poor Maeve."

"Well, we stared too when we first saw her," I muttered.

"Not like that. And Kitty wrinkled up her nose as if she smelled something bad. Honestly, I could have smacked her."

I slammed the refrigerator door, which didn't make me feel any better because it made no noise. Mom was just like Jo-Jo and all the other females. It made no difference what age they were. Just because Kitty was super-looking, they picked on her.

"And I don't know about the beach tomorrow either," Mom said.

I had my own doubts about it. We'd arranged to go to Santa Monica for the day, all day. Dad was lending me the car, and Tom, my best friend, was coming. And Kitty. Just the four of us.

"Maeve will have to be really careful, or she'll burn," Mom said. "And I don't want her going out too far into the surf. She thinks she's a better swimmer than she is."

"She could walk to Catalina Island without getting her head underwater," I mumbled, which was mean because she wasn't that tall. And besides, none of this was her fault.

"I think your Dad and I better go too," Mom said.

"Are you kidding?" She couldn't be serious. But she was. It ended up with me promising to watch Maeve every second. To not let her go in the ocean alone. To bring a beach umbrella. A beach umbrella! It hardly seemed worth the hassle.

Tom called that night. "I hear she's a real weirdo," he said.

"Who told you that?"

"A munchkin." I knew who the munchkin was all right. I lowered my voice. In this house more than the walls had ears. "Listen. When she gets a tan Maeve will be terrific."

"Oh yeah? That's not what I heard. I guess

I'll see for myself tomorrow."

I had a lot of mixed feelings about tomorrow, and I woke up half hoping it was raining. But of course it wasn't. It never rains in southern California. Everybody knows that.

Dad had already been to the 24-hour drugstore, and he'd bought Maeve a tube of sun screen junk and a big hat. He helped me wedge the beach umbrella into the back seat.

Maeve wore jeans and the blue shirt. The blue and pink string of her swimsuit looped over the back collar. She cradled the hat and the brown sun screen tube. I fixed my surfboard on the roof rack with room beside it for Tom's.

"Have a good time," Mom said. She put an arm around Jo-Jo, who was sulking because she couldn't come.

"Bye," I said, and I drove slowly down the street till we turned the corner onto Valley Boulevard. Then I speeded up.

"Tell me about Tom," Maeve said.

I sensed an uneasiness in her that hadn't been there at home. Last night we'd sat out by the pool and talked. All of us. Maeve had told us about Ireland and the school where she had to wear a uniform with a white shirt and a tie. "It's to try to make us all look the same," she'd explained. Jo-Jo's eyes had bugged out, and she'd said, "You mean all the girls over there look like you?"

Maeve had been the first one to laugh. "Pity help the poor things if they did," she'd said.

Maeve had even played a few Irish tunes for us on her harmonica, which she called a mouth organ. She'd been at ease with us. But she wasn't at ease now.

"Well, Tom is my best friend," I said. "We're both on the surfing team."

"Will I be able to see you do that today?"

"Sure." It was amazing how I could understand her accent now. I understood everything she said, just about.

"There's Kitty's house," I said.

Kitty came running out when I beeped, and I felt myself begin to sweat. Kitty could make me sweatier than any girl I'd ever met.

I got out, and she put an arm around my waist and smiled into the car at Maeve. Then she saw the beach umbrella, and her nose wrinkled. As if she smelled something bad! I put Mom's words out of my head. Kitty had a cute nose. It was even cuter when she turned it up like that. "What's that for?" she asked. "Somebody's grandmother?"

I tried to laugh it off. "Oh, Mom is afraid Maeve might burn." I opened the back door for her, and she said, "Great! And I get to sit with it." She sort of slid underneath it. "We aren't really going to take it on the beach, though, are we, Eric? We'll look like a bunch of geeks."

"I'm sorry," Maeve said.

I felt a sudden irritation. So what if beach umbrellas weren't too cool? Sometimes there were things you had to do.

Kitty sat forward. I smelled her rose perfume, and I wished she and I were going to the beach alone.

"I was only kidding," she said.

I smiled. "I know."

Tom waited with his surfboard for us in his front yard. He looked at Maeve and then raised his eyebrows at Kitty. Kitty giggled.

Dad wouldn't have approved of the way I gunned the motor as soon as Tom got his board stashed on the roof.

I could see him and Kitty each time I looked in the rearview mirror. They were sitting awfully close. I knew it was because of the umbrella, but still it bugged me. Sometimes they said things to each other that I couldn't hear.

Maeve hardly talked at all, and I noticed she closed her eyes while we were going through the interchange. When we zoomed through the tunnel and got the first glimpse of the ocean sparkling blue beyond its stretch of sand, I asked, "Nice?"

"Lovely," Maeve said. I'd noticed already that "lovely" was her super superlative word.

The day got off to a bad start. As soon as I stuck the umbrella in the sand, Kitty and Tom moved to lie away from us. Later, when I walked Maeve down to the edge of the water, both of us had to brave the stares. Maeve bit her lips.

"Don't let them bother you," I said, but I had to admit that she looked whiter than ever here where everyone was already tanned to the color of toast.

We watched the towels and stuff while Kitty and Tom swam.

"Don't you want to go in with them again?" Maeve asked.

I shook my head and lay down on my stomach. I couldn't leave her sitting here alone. What a bummer today had been. What a bummer the whole summer would be.

The waves came up in the afternoon, and Tom and I got in some surfing.

"I knew she was weird," Tom said as we paddled out. "But you might have warned me that she was a Moby Dick."

"What do you mean, a Moby Dick?"

He grinned at me. "A white whale, dummy."

I looked back and saw Maeve sitting under the umbrella. Kitty still lay at a distance.

Some guy had stopped and was talking to her. I was sick of other guys talking to Kitty. She was my girl. I leaned across and shoved Tom off his board.

He came up sputtering. "What did you do that for?"

"Why don't you shut up about Maeve," I said, and I paddled furiously ahead of him.

But later, sitting on my board with nobody around but the seagulls, I faced the truth. The joy in knocking Tom off had come from the memory of how he'd been in the car with Kitty. It had nothing to do with Maeve, so I realized I should quit feeling that I was such a heck of a guy.

When we got home, Mom was pleased that Maeve didn't have a burn.

"The way you're coddling her, she'll be white as a dove till the day she leaves," I told her.

Mom looked thoughtful. "Maybe ten minutes a day in the backyard," she said.

"Look," I said. "You better do something. It isn't easy for her being the only strange-looking chick around."

For the next few days Mom timed Maeve's backyard sunning the way she'd time an egg she was cooking. "Over," she'd call, and Maeve would turn to toast the other side.

But it wasn't any good. She got pink, and then the pink faded back to the original white. Once she stayed out for half an hour, but she blistered, so we could see that that wouldn't work.

I spent a lot of time with her, and I had to admit she was interesting. She tried to explain to me about the Irish religious thing, and she told me about the records they listened to over there and the TV programs that they watched. She was funny, too. She couldn't believe the way our yard sprinklers popped up out of the ground. And she thought we were crazy in the first place—watering grass! Each night she played her harmonica. She played as if she heard things the rest of us couldn't hear, knew things the rest of us couldn't know. Even Jo-Jo stayed quiet when Maeve played.

"You're a fairy," Dad said in his fake Irish accent. "One of the wee folk."

"Oh, I'm wee all right. A wee giant," Maeve answered in her fake American one.

Twice when I called Kitty, she wasn't home. But she and Tom were going with us to the Fourth of July fireworks at the Rose Bowl. I'd had the tickets even before Maeve had come.

It was a super summer night. "Lovely," as Maeve would say.

When we went out to Dad's car, she got in the back seat. "So Kitty can be next to you," she said. "I'm feeling bad about the two of you."

"Don't," I said. But the thought of Kitty sitting next to me added a new glow to the evening.

Kitty wore a blue sundress that left her honey-colored shoulders bare. She got in beside me. "Hi, Eric. Maeve."

"Hello," Maeve said, and I knew her well enough by now to sense the way she was tightening up.

Tom didn't sit real close to her when he got in the car. He was probably wishing he had Kitty back there with him. I turned on some music and let it fill the car.

We parked outside the Rose Bowl and walked. When we got to our seats, I worked it so that I was between the girls. Unfortunately, Tom was on Kitty's other side, but there wasn't much I could do about that.

There was always a circus before the fireworks to allow time for it to get dark. Maeve grabbed for my hand when the guy on the trapeze made his first leap, and it would have been kind of unfriendly to turn her hand loose when he was safe. I held on.

I hoped Kitty wouldn't notice. Then I noticed something myself. Tom was holding her hand. What a nerve, when she was my girl and he was my friend.

Dark was falling now, drifting in behind the mountains, dropping onto the soft green turf. First stars sparkled in the sky. I reached down and found Kitty's soft little hand, and I felt really romantic for a minute . . . till I pictured the four of us in a chain, all holding on to each other. Some romance!

The firemen set their displays up, and soon the first blue starburst dazzled across the sky.

Boom! Boom! Rockets exploded around

us, and suddenly I felt Maeve throw herself against me. Her arms were tight around my neck, her head buried in my chest. She was shaking.

"Maeve!" I released my other hand from Kitty's.

Maeve began to whimper, and then she pulled away. I saw the white blur of her face before she turned, trampling her way out over people's feet.

I stood up.

"Honestly! What now?" Kitty asked.

I pushed out behind Maeve, and I caught up with her in the exit tunnel. She was running with her hands pressed tight against her ears. I got an arm around her. "What is it? What's wrong?"

"It's the noise. Like bombs," she whispered. "Like guns." When another rocket exploded, she cringed against the wall.

"I'll take you home," I said, and I held her close till the shaking stopped.

"But what about Kitty and Tom?"

"I'll come back for them."

"No. It's all right. I'll be fine in a minute."

We ended up watching from the car with the windows tightly closed to keep out part of the noise and my arm around Maeve for protection. She seemed to enjoy the fireworks that way. Once she said, "Oh, lovely," when a crimson-tailed comet flared across the sky, so I knew she was enjoying it. The lights in the sky turned her hair to flame, and when her cheek touched mine, it was as soft as a flower.

I took my arm away when the crowd started coming out. We watched for Tom and Kitty.

"Having a good time?" Kitty asked, and I saw her look at Maeve. Maeve's natural was flattened on one side where our heads had been pressed together.

"What was that all about?" Tom asked.

"Nothing," I said, and I couldn't decide how I felt when he and Kitty got in the back seat together.

I didn't hear from Kitty for three days after that. Then she called and said, "You haven't forgotten my birthday, have you, Eric? Day after tomorrow?"

How could I forget? I'd already bought her a silver heart on a chain with money I'd taken from my next-summer-surfing-in-Hawaii fund.

"I'm having a pool party," she said.

"How come? You don't have a pool."

Kitty giggled. "It's at Sasha's." Sasha was

Kitty's cousin. "You're invited."

There was a pause. Then I asked, "How about Maeve?"

"Maeve too. I didn't expect you'd come without her. About three."

"I'm not sure," Maeve said when I told her. "Why don't you go by yourself, Eric."

"Too bad she had to make it a pool party this year." Mom looked at me suspiciously. "Why did she, Eric?"

"I don't know." But I did know why Maeve wasn't sure about going. There'd be all those eyes again. Everyone staring. New kids too. Ones she hadn't met before.

But the next day Maeve was really chipper. "I'm having my hair cut tomorrow morning," she said. "For the party. Your mom knows a place where they're good with hair like mine."

I wondered where in the world Mom had found a place like that!

"I was afraid to suggest it before in case she would be offended," Mom whispered to me when Maeve and Jo-Jo were playing ping-pong. "But she wasn't."

She and Maeve went off the next morning about 11, and Jo-Jo disappeared somewhere on her bicycle.

Maeve did look really good when she got back, her hair curling in short, feathery curls around her face.

"Hey, foxy lady!" I said and watched her cheeks get pink.

Jo-Jo waved a small paper sack. "You look super, Maeve. And I've bought you a present too."

"It's not my birthday," Maeve told her.

"Upstairs, upstairs. It's a secret," Jo-Jo said.

"Don't be long," I warned. "Tom is picking us up in a half hour."

I fixed myself a quick second lunch and

got into my swimsuit. I rolled the little gift box in my towel, and I hoped there'd be a chance to see Kitty alone. I banged on Maeve's door. "Hurry up in there!"

I waited for her on the front steps.

She came out slowly, wearing blue jeans and a long-sleeved shirt.

"Aren't you going to be hot?" I asked. "Where's your suit?"

"Underneath." Her eyes slid away from mine. "But I think I'll just keep my clothes on."

I nodded, thinking I understood. That way the eyes would be easier on her. "Got your mouth organ?" I asked.

"Yes." There was something odd about her that I couldn't figure.

"You don't have to play it, you know, if you don't want to," I said. Bringing the harmonica had been Mom's idea. "It'll do those kids good to hear how talented Maeve is," she said. "They think they're so darn superior."

"Your hair is lovely," I teased, trying to make her smile. But even my teasing didn't work. And there was something about me that was puzzling too. I missed that big, red natural. Now that it was gone, I wished we'd just left her the way she was.

Tom whistled when he saw the new hairdo, and I knew it did make a difference. So what was the matter with me?

We were late to the party. Music was already blasting from Sasha's backyard. Kids were splashing in the pool. There were good smells of hamburgers and hot dogs barbecuing.

Maeve sat in the shade of an avocado tree with the lemonade. She was the only who wasn't swimming.

"Aren't you dying in this heat?" Kitty asked her, but Maeve shook her head.

I went over to talk to her a couple of times, but I was busy myself having fun most of the time. There was a sleepy kind of lull in the late afternoon. I looked at Maeve sitting by herself in the shade, and my conscience jumped up and bit me.

"Hey, you guys," I said. "You ought to hear the way Maeve plays the harmonica."

Someone giggled. "The harmonica?"

"Yeah. Come on, Maeve. Play for us."

Maeve took out her mouth organ.

I'd heard her play lots of times. But never like that. There was such sadness in her music, such loneliness. Everybody was suddenly quiet. I guess what that music did was make us think about ourselves. The kids began drifting across to sit around her under the tree. I didn't know what she was playing. It could have been about the "troubles," or maybe it was a sad love story. I didn't know. I did know that she cast a spell.

I looked across at Kitty, and I saw something in her face that I couldn't believe. Kitty was jealous! Couldn't be. But she was. It was only for an instant. Then she saw me looking, and at the same time, Maeve stopped playing.

"More, Maeve, more," the kids yelled.

Maeve wiped a hand across her forehead and smiled. "I'm awfully hot," she said.

"Well, have a swim." Kitty jumped up and yelled, "Grab an arm somebody. Let's dump her."

The kids began laughing and dragging Maeve to the pool.

I grinned. They weren't being mean. It was a good sign. We all did that to each other. Maybe they were accepting her at last.

"Get her jeans off," Kitty shouted, and that was OK too. She had her swimsuit on, and this way she'd have dry clothes for later.

"Eric!" Maeve yelled, and I saw suddenly

that she was panicked. I ran across, fighting to get through to her. But I was too late.

Someone had pulled her shirt off. Someone else had tugged her foot clear of her jeans.

I saw the blue and pink swimsuit. And something else. Then I heard the burst of laughter.

Maeve stood, all hunched over. Her left leg and left arm were a bright, startling orange.

She snatched up her clothes and began running.

I caught up with her halfway along Sasha's street. "Hey, wait," I said. "I seem to be spending my summer chasing after you."

She was sobbing, great hiccupy sobs. She wouldn't talk to me till she pulled on her jeans and shirt.

"Jo-Jo bought me this stuff," she said. Her eyes were misty, and I found myself thinking of dumb things like bluebells in the rain. Especially dumb because I'd never seen a bluebell, wet or dry.

"It was supposed to make me tan. She did one leg. I did my arm. When we saw what was happening, it was too late."

"Oh, that Jo-Jo," I said. "I'll wring her neck."

"It wasn't her fault. She was just trying to make me be like everyone else."

I looked at her, and something strange was happening. I was melting. I was turning all soft and squashy. "But I don't want you to be like everyone else," I said. "You're special."

"I am?"

"Yes." I heard the truth in my voice, and I put my arms around her and pushed my face into her short, red curls.

We sat on the curb. Maeve jerked up one leg of her jeans and made a face. "Will this come off? I don't want to be that special."

We laughed together.

"Mom will know some way." I took her hand, and I couldn't remember ever feeling so terrific. The summer stretched ahead, filled with days we would spend together. "I hear there are some great waves at a place called Boogaloo Bay in Ireland," I said dreamily. "Is that far from you?"

"No place is far from another place over there," Maeve said. "And Boogaloo Bay is in the south. The part that gets no bombs."

"I think I'll come there next summer," I said. "Your hair will have grown out. Hawaii can wait."

"They'll all be staring at you, and you riding the tops of the waves like that," Maeve said.

"Who cares? I'll come anyway."

Maeve squeezed my hand. "Och, Eric," she said. "You're lovely, just lovely."

Canyon Ridge High
School Library